EDDIE

Jae Carvel

United States 2017

Cover Design by Gwen Gades
Edited by Mary Menke

*This is a work of fiction. Names, characters, places, brands, media, and incidents are
either the product of the author's imagination or are used fictitiously. Any resemblance to
similarly named places or to persons living or deceased is unintentional.*

PROLOGUE

Eddie
1897-1942

Whatever happened to Eddie Martin?

At age 19, Eddie Martin has a brutal fight with his high school teacher and leaves home. The first two books in the Strawberry Mountain Series, *By the River* and *Secrets from the Little Red Box*, leave readers wondering about Eddie, the youngest son of Sarah Ann and Thomas Martin. He journeys from the ranch in the Upper John Day Valley into the Blue Mountains where Strawberry Butte is the tallest and most beautiful in the range. Fear of being searched out by the sheriff, forces him to keep going.

Eddie loves his family, protects their good name and regrets his bad decisions. As he recovers from his mistakes, he applies his childhood lessons to his adult life. He is a young man who must look over his shoulder to see if he is being pursued throughout his travels...travels that take him from the John Day Valley to the Malheur Valley where he changes his name to Jim Drake. He crosses the Oregon Desert, goes over the Cascades to Gold Beach, then Ashland, and then north to the Palouse country of Washington, Priest Lake in Idaho, and halfway across the continent to Nebraska. It takes most of his life for him to discover the truth of the man he has become.

This book is dedicated to Joann, Bob, David, and Robbie, who listened so patiently.

AUTHOR INFORMATION

Jae Carvel's Strawberry Mountain Series is inspired by the tales of her pioneer ancestors, which pique her imagination as she writes another story that could be true, or not. She is a retired junior high teacher who shares her East Wenatchee home with her husband where they enjoy drop-ins from their children and grandchildren. No matter what the era, Jae believes people solve their problems in about the same way from generation to generation...always hoping to somehow make life better with their efforts.

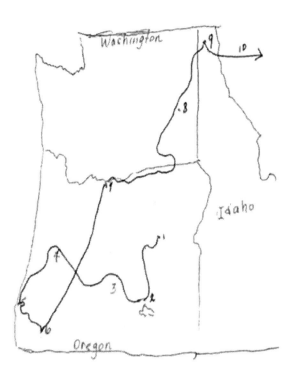

Washington

Idaho

Oregon

EDDIE'S TRAVELS

CHAPTER ONE

EVERYBODY KNOWS you don't shove Eddie Martin.

For Eddie's senior paper, he chose a controversial topic for 1895: "Women Should/Should Not Have the Right to Vote in Oregon." Mr. Page, the teacher, came down on the side of "should not." Eddie's mother thought "should" was long overdue. Eddie had even quoted from some of his mother's reading material in his paper.

Eddie Martin has a bright mind, but I can force him to change his point of view with the stroke of my pen, thought the teacher. He knew the F would rankle the boy, but maybe it would get him to change his thinking. After all, a teacher should teach more than just grammar and organization. Content is important. Eddie should show more than one point of view in a paper of this nature. When women get the vote, things will change.

At the end of class, after most students had left school, Eddie stormed to the front of the room to challenge the grade on his final paper.

Mr. Page said, "Read my comments. The grade stands." He put his right hand on Eddie's chest and pushed him toward the door.

"All my papers are correctly written. So is this one! This'll keep me from getting my diploma. You're doing this on purpose!" shouted Eddie.

"I am doing this to get you to think properly," began the teacher just as Eddie brought the conversation to a close with his punch to the teacher's nose.

It was a hell of a fight that left the teacher motionless in the dirt. A man like Mr. Page, who had spent most of his life with his nose in a book, avoiding physical pursuits and schoolyard fights as a boy, was no match for his student. Eddie, at nineteen, had stood his ground with his three older brothers, done his ranch chores under duress, and backed up his bad-tempered decisions with fisticuffs. Yet, people who knew his true spirit would find him reading books, newspapers and even poetry in his spare time. His senior paper was a venture into political writing and Mr. Page had crushed it with the F. Defeat on the paper brought Eddie to his other way to solve problems, one punch after another in a blind rage. Graduating from the new Prairie City High School was an important goal and the skinny, opinionated teacher had ruined his dream. Eddie's punches to his head had put him to the ground.

Mr. Page had landed some painful blows, but Eddie had been surprised at how easily the man had crumpled in the dirt of the schoolyard. When he quit moving, townspeople came running. Someone yelled, "Get the doc!" and Eddie grabbed his horse and mounted up as soon as he saw help coming. Deep inside, he harbored the nagging fear that the teacher was seriously injured. He crawled into his saddle and headed for the ranch, hanging to the saddle horn for support. He wiped blood and snot from his nose. Pain in his ribs made it difficult to take deep breaths.

Eddie held on as Dauber turned down the lane, ears perked up as horses do when headed for the barn. Clint's horse, Drumstick, was standing at the gate to the yard. One could always count on classmate Clint to spread the word when there was news in town. Today the news was Eddie's fight with Mr. Page. Clint had explained to Thomas and Sarah Ann that Eddie had been in a fight with the teacher. Clint's opinion was that Mr. Page had failed Eddie on his final paper and Eddie felt it was unfairly marked.

Then Clint and Thomas looked up and saw Eddie on Dauber, coming down the lane. When Pa saw how badly Eddie was hurt, he signaled for Clint to help him get his son to the house. Ma and sister Evelyn began tending him and Clint removed himself, knowing there would be private family talk before long. The family heard Eddie's details of the fight before he dropped off to sleep.

"Sarah Ann, this doesn't sound good to me. I expect we will hear from the law before tomorrow is over," said Thomas.

"This boy is so easily provoked," observed Sarah Ann. "His quick temper draws him into trouble, even if it is justified."

"Beating a man to within an inch of his life is never justified." Thomas held strong opinions about fighting. "When you pray tonight, just beg that Mr. Page recovers."

Sarah Ann prayed, but she slept very little.

Upstairs, Eddie spent a fitful night as well. *I think I'll make myself scarce,* he thought when he rose from his restless sleep. Before the rest of the family got up to do chores, he fashioned a bedroll from his blankets, filled a knapsack with necessary items such as matches, his compass, leather gloves, binoculars, jerky and dried fruit. From under his bed he drew a fat wallet stuffed with all his money. He was very glad he had been a thrifty packrat during his high school years.

The usual whiffs of breakfast floated up the stairs to his room, so he limped his way to the kitchen for some of his ma's biscuits and gravy. As the family was eating, they heard hooves on the lane, and Clint rapped on the back porch door. "Howdy, folks. I thought I should let you know. It's all over town this morning. Mr. Page died last night." Clint took a very long pause. "The sheriff is expected in town before the day is over. I guess he'll want to talk to Eddie, to see if it was self-defense."

Every Martin around the table lost his or her appetite. The color drained from Sarah Ann's face.

"You better ride down and meet him. It will look better if you do," advised Thomas.

"I don't think so, Pa. I won't be here when he comes, either," Eddie said.

"Ma, can I take some of those biscuits with me? They're the tastiest you've ever made," said Eddie as he gave her a little hug.

Eddie saddled Dauber, tied his bedroll and pack behind his saddle, and would not be dissuaded from riding up the river. His ma and pa and Evelyn, his frightened younger sister, watched him ride until he disappeared around the bend. When he was sure to be out of sight from the house, Eddie turned south toward the mountain. He felt less likely to be followed by going over the rugged wilderness of Strawberry.

Back in the barnyard, Sarah Ann called her son George over. "Eddie rode off, stubborn as usual. He says he's not coming back. Would you saddle up and go after him? He may have cooled down a bit and be willing to come home."

"Ma, you know he doesn't listen to me. I'll go after him, but please don't keep your hopes up," said George. "Which way did he go?"

"He headed east, going over Toll Gate, I imagine. That's the easiest way out of the valley."

True, Eddie had hoped the family would think his plans would take him east. He and Dauber covered ground to the south quickly and quietly, getting out of sight from any family pursuers.

CHAPTER TWO

SHORTLY AFTER TURNING SOUTH, Eddie and Dauber crossed the John Day River. Dauber took a long drink and enjoyed a bit of fresh grass from the bank. Eddie filled his canteen from a spot where a spring flowed into the river. Before mounting up again, he noticed a shady, damp place where he and his mother had often come to pick watercress. Eddie loved watercress, so he quickly gathered some to stuff in his mouth and some more to put in his biscuit and jerky sandwich. He then headed on through Johnson's field, cut across Albert's hill pasture and took the backside into the ranches that lined Strawberry creek. He stayed near the brush along the creek hoping he would not be seen. Dauber was a beautiful, unusual-colored pinto that would be recognized by many who lived in the valley. Eddie hoped he would not be forced to trade Dauber to keep from being spotted. The lump in his throat grew as Eddie realized there was a lot involved with this leaving business, not like when he was a little kid who planned to run away from home.

The Avery Place was the last ranch up Strawberry Creek. It sat on the tree line of the mountain. Paul and Ella were longtime acquaintances of the Martins. Eddie felt safe in asking if he could spend the night in their barn. Paul was curious and invited Eddie to stay for dinner. The story came out as they shared their meal with Eddie.

In the morning they tried every means possible to convince Eddie to go back and face the music. "The sheriff will be open to self-defense, I'm sure," urged Paul. They could see the stubborn young man would not change his mind. After breakfast, they filled his lunch sack with leftovers and found an unused oilcloth to tie over his bedroll and backpack.

"At least he won't go hungry or get wet today," sighed Ella as he rode off.

"I guess I'll have to ride to town later today and report that we've seen him; that is if the law is looking for him," mused Paul. "I think I'll stop at Thomas Martin's place first and see what the news is."

"Oh, that's a good idea," said Ella. "Sarah Ann must be beside herself with worry."

CHAPTER THREE

EDDIE AND DAUBER LEFT THE AVERY'S and worked their way up Strawberry Creek. The spring temperature at this high altitude nipped at any exposed bare skin. Eddie took the leather gloves out of the pack and put them on, holding Dauber's reins as the pair picked their way through brushy spots trying not to break limbs or leave tracks that could be followed. It made for slow going until an occasional bare spot appeared where they could smartly step out and cover ground. But those spots captured rays of sun and added warmth. Snow still clung to shady spots, which enhanced the light-drenched spaces even more.

After a full morning of climbing, the onion fields came into sight. The early season produced only tiny new shoots, but Eddie could smell the distinctive odor of onions, and he pictured his mother's kitchen table with pot roast, carrots, potatoes, and onions cooling on the counter until the family and hired hands came in for the noon meal. He sighed and buried the memory before dismounting and giving Dauber some grazing time. Eddie pulled some onion sprouts to add to the remnants of his watercress-enhanced sandwich. Satisfying and tasty, the noon respite gave the man and horse incentive to move on.

They headed east from the onion fields in a zig-zag pattern that took them up the face of the mountain. Fir, spruce, and tamarack cast shade over the semblance of a trail they followed. Near the end of daylight, they came upon a clearing. As if by magic, Eddie could see the whole of the upper John Day Valley. Every creek glistened in the sunset. The various barns at each place spoke the truth of the ranches that dotted the landscape. Eddie could name the owners of each that he could see. The little town filled a larger spot to the left of the scene before him. Then he thought, *The sheriff is probably in Prairie City asking questions about me and the fight, and the death of Mr. Page. He has probably gone out to the ranch to talk to the folks and look for me. I am sorry this will be so hard on my ma.*

The darkening sky warned Eddie he should find a camping spot before long. He located a spot near a spring with an outcropping of rocks and a fringe of brush. At this point, he investigated his pack and was much relieved to see Ella Avery's bar of lye soap, something he had forgotten in his haste to leave the ranch. It would mean clean hands and eating utensils as long as he was on the road. Tomorrow he would stop at the lake, a real chance to get cleaned up.

The oilcloth made a good barrier to the damp ground, and Eddie spread out his bedroll. He built a little twig fire that would not put out enough smoke to be seen, and heated a little of his food. When he got out of sight of the valley, he would need to find game and actually do some cooking, maybe in a day or two. Emotions filled him: a longing for his family, regret over the fight, excitement for the adventure ahead of him.

Eddie had not decided what he wanted to do with his life even when his parents kept asking him. Now the decisions were being thrust upon him. The stress of thinking and the weariness of mountain climbing brought sleep to the "boy becoming man" at the end of his second day.

*   *   *

"Brrr," said Eddie through his chattering teeth. He stirred around in his twig fire bed and managed enough spark to heat up his tin cup of water. He finished off another biscuit, spread dirt over the fire and saddled Dauber. He led the horse to where a steep trail began. Eddie had made this climb before on summer trips to Strawberry Lake. It was steep for a man and even more so for a packed horse, so he decided to climb beside Dauber, his companion. Dauber exhaled a horse "harrumph," as the climbing got steep and tough. They took a rest after the first half mile, then tackled the steepest part, which still sported slippery patches of snow in the shady spots. Their hard work was rewarded when the lake came into view. Some icy edges remained, but the clear, sunny sky shown true blue and reflected in the cobalt blue of the lake.

Eddie had worked up a sweat with the climb, so he removed one of the layers of clothing he had enjoyed putting on when he woke this morning. He had even decided that tonight he would wear an extra layer to bed. Back at the ranch, Ma made everyone wait until twelve o'clock to eat the noon meal. Eddie decided that was not the case here and that he had earned time for a few pants to catch his breath while he snacked on some jerky. He chose a seat on the outcropping of rocks at the base of the lake. Two chipmunks also called this home as they scampered about. Eddie eyed them but decided they were far too cute and too small to eat. More sensibly, he chose to rescue his line and hooks from his pack and try his hand at fishing. With luck, this leaving home could be fun, as long as Sheriff Logan didn't figure where he has headed on his fishing trip.

He found a branch and tied his line to it so he could fling it farther into the lake. It would be best if he could wade out a ways to drop his hook, but wet boots would be a real challenge for a man on the move. Eddie realized that is what he was. He pulled his pocket watch from his pocket to verify that what seemed like dinner time was actually 11:30. With three trout hanging from his forked stick, it was time to cook. He started another fire, this one in a spot that other hikers and campers used. While it heated up, Eddie used his hunting knife to clean the fish and then string them out over the fire. He buried the innards to cover his tracks, and waited for his dinner, not as good as battered and fried, but far beyond wonderful for the hungry young man.

Dauber carried Eddie and their belongings to the far end of the lake. A bit of a meadow provided Dauber's treat in a swampy area. Beyond that, shale lay on the hillside, looking like sizeable crystals sliding to the lake's edge. On a sunny day like this one, the rocks were warmed, even in May. Eddie chose the edge of the shale slide for his evening camp. He staked Dauber in the brush to the south so he wouldn't be spotted by any early camper coming to Strawberry Lake just for the fun of it, or for the purpose of looking for a runaway man, guilty of murder. The dreams of trouble led to a restless night as the warmed shale became cold and hard to sleep on. Morning would be a time for some serious planning.

CHAPTER FOUR

BACK AT THE RANCH, Sarah Ann could not escape the turmoil of her missing son being wanted for murder. In church on Sunday, the whole congregation had prayed for Eddie's return and that Mr. Page would recover, as he hung on to life by a thread. Fortunately, Clint's report of Mr. Page dying had been wrong, but Sarah Ann could still feel the hot breath of gossip as they left church, and she told Thomas she would not be able to go again.

Evelyn felt some excitement at the notoriety of it all, but her mother's grief overshadowed her feelings. She knew Eddie had been well prepared when he left home. As long as she could remember, he had supplies stored under his bed, in case he got mad at his brothers and decided to leave home. It began when he was a little boy, but just became a habit as he got older. Then when he worked summer jobs at other ranches and earned money, most of it went into the coffee tin under the bed, way back where no one could find it.

Only Evelyn knew, as she was his little sister and confidant and never a threat. She missed him already but never feared that he would not be able to take care of himself. Evelyn knew it: Eddie was tough as nails.

*   *   *

The day after Eddie left, Paul Avery rode by on his way to town. It was curious that he came out of his way to get to town. He was invited in, but just stood on the porch and talked to Thomas before he rode on. He did tell Thomas that he had seen the boy, but he did not feel inclined to spread the word or look up Sheriff Logan. "If Page actually dies, I will come forward with the lawful information," Paul assured Thomas. "We are all law abiding in this valley, but I see no reason to rush about it." Thomas decided to let Sarah Ann get some of her grieving out of the way before he shared Paul's message.

"Thomas, if Mr. Page pulls through, do you think the law will still be after Eddie?" asked Sarah Ann as they finished their supper.

Evelyn was all ears as she listened to her parents' conversation. She had watched him riding Dauber east on his way to Toll Gate Pass. Eddie would be halfway to Idaho by now if she calculated correctly. This crime committed in Oregon would surely be of no consequence in another state. Her knowledge of the law was sketchy, to say the least. Eddie could stop by Amy's place on the border. No one there would turn him in. Evelyn pictured plans for her brother that would take him to safety and eventually back together with his family.

Evelyn's father was not as optimistic about his son's future. Eddie had fueled his reputation as a hothead who would rather fight than reason out his disagreements. Thomas recalled when he decided a strong hand was needed with the boy. He had made mental plans to improve Eddie's attitude, for the boy's benefit. He also remembered that most of his efforts were unsuccessful.

Sarah Ann had better luck with her son as he grew up with an interest in books, writing his ideas, and leaning toward the political thoughts of the day. He found injustice in the world that was nearing a new century. Pa was afraid he might want to be a lawyer, something in which he could not imagine supporting his son. He had helped his other children get land and become ranchers. Eddie was a different breed. He didn't even want land—too much trouble. Eddie was an idea man.

CHAPTER FIVE

JUNE 1 BROKE BRIGHT AGAIN at Strawberry Lake. Eddie's enjoyment of fishing and camping could have lasted longer, but he heard conversation across the lake, which sat in a mile-wide bowl that shared echoes from all sides. Eddie slipped behind the brush at the far end near the swamp and prayed Dauber would not choose to whinny. The voices moved east toward the Slide Lake trail, and Eddie gave a sigh of relief. However, it was a wake-up call to get on with his plans. June 1 reminded him that hunters and fisherman would be combing the area for fun and food. He also realized he should mark dates somewhere in his pack, count the days so months would not pass him by.

His best meal so far had been rabbit, which he cleaned and roasted over his campfire. He had no plans to hunt larger game as it would be too hard for a man on the run to dispose of remains. Before leaving camp, he put Ella's lye soap to good use, cleaning himself and his few utensils. Eddie was well-read and knew the advantages to cleanliness for health reasons, if for no other. His mother had always made him wash behind his ears, so that habit stuck with him.

Of all the things he forgot to bring on this trip, he missed reading material the most. At home he could always be found behind a tree in the orchard shirking the duty of chores with a magazine or newspaper pulled from his hip pocket. Reading surpassed the grief of being reprimanded by his father. "If I ever get out of this pickle, Dauber, I'll earn some money and read for a law degree." Then he realized, he would not have a diploma of graduation. He blew that chance with his first punch on Mr. Page's nose.

He mounted Dauber and headed up the mountain toward Little Strawberry Lake, a jewel in a pocket of shale. It was worth a poem, if only he had pencil and paper. Then he remembered: Ella had wrapped his soap in paper, and there was a school pencil with a broken lead in his overalls' pocket. Eddie and Dauber stopped for a breather, he took his knife out to sharpen the pencil, and wrote the first of his travel poems:

"The Center of Little Strawberry Lake"
The center sparkles

Like jewels of a rich lady's ring
The darkness of edges
Like a muddy protector
Keeps it safe
To wink in the sunlight forever.
June 1, 1895

Eddie heard early spring birds twittering and chirping, rustling their wings at their mates as they located places for their nests. Then he heard running water, lots of it. For the first time, Eddie discovered beautiful Strawberry Falls. Creek water spilled over a high bank, splashing nearly forty feet into a pool before flowing on out. Nature had built a wonder, better than any man. The perfect shower, which Eddie would have used if he had not cleaned up already this morning. He took his compass from his pack and set about determining exactly where the falls cascaded over the rocky outcrop and what direction they were from Little Strawberry Lake. Eddie was headed into deeper woods, out of sight, but he planned to revisit this spot before he left the mountain for good. He had not decided just when that would be, but certainly before the late fall storms buttoned the area under glaciers and wind drifted snow. Three months of roaming and exploring lay ahead, and Eddie pushed his troubles to the back of his brain and mounted Dauber one more time.

The pair began climbing. The big firs were replaced by scrawny pines and tamaracks. Brush was shorter, unable to create a hiding place. Coming around a bend in the trail, Dauber shied and Eddie grabbed his saddle horn just to stay mounted. An owl as huge as Eddie had ever seen flapped its giant wings and swooshed by, no doubt hunting for tiny animals to prey upon. A landscape of rocks blocked their path, and Eddie decided to head down the mountain for a time. There was no need to summit the top today. It wasn't going anywhere. High Lake had a reputation for good fishing, but few fishermen took the extra time to get there on a day trip. It seemed as if it might be a good place to camp for the month of June. So the young man and his horse set out again with a goal in mind.

They arrived at High Lake just before sundown. There was a feeling of rain in the air, a perfect time for fishing. In fact, fish were jumping and splashing. Eddie remembered that back at the ranch, they'd go out to the river to fish if it felt like a rain storm was coming, so it seemed like a good time to try here. There were no signs of people or abandoned camps, convincing Eddie that he was right to assume it was too early for people to come to the mountain. He arranged his campsite in a spot where he could get a view of the lake and the trail that approached it. He caught enough trout to string a line for drying. He might be able to coax enough smoke from his fire to smoke the fish. He could then pack them and carry them when he decided to venture about.

CHAPTER SIX

THE NEXT DAY, sitting on the edge of the lake, Eddie began noticing new plants. They reminded him of a book from the school library he had studied to learn the names of all the plants in the woods around Prairie City. He located huckleberry brush just leafing out. Next month they would sport little white blossoms, and by the middle of August, the red berries would be ready for picking. Eddie could eat a gallon of huckleberries in one sitting, but he knew he could also dry them and carry them with his smoked fish when he left camp. Then there was the danger of bears who liked huckleberries as much as Eddie did, just a reminder to stay alert. Every day he would spot more wildflowers, glacier lilies, Indian paint brush, yarrow, and on and on.

About the third week in June, weather was warm and sunny. Eddie decided this was the right time to put the lye soap to good use and to wash his bedding and clothes. He did the scrubbing first thing in the morning and spread the laundry out on the sun-warmed rocks on the edge of High Lake. While the clothes dried, he took Dauber to the far side of the lake for some good grazing. Dauber seemed to be enjoying his treat of new grass when he raised his head, and his ears pointed forward. Eddie grabbed his horse's mouth to prevent the whinny that was about to escape. On a lower trail, Eddie spotted three riders heading east, concentrating on their destination, and not looking toward High Lake. Eddie and Dauber slipped into the brush until the riders disappeared.

"Well, Dauber, I sure let my guard down. Life at our camp has been too easy. As soon as the clothes dry, we'll pack up. I need to have everything ready to go at a moment's notice and to keep our camp out of sight after every day." Some days Eddie found himself talking to his horse as if he were a human companion.

If the weather continued to improve until the end of June, they could count on visitors by July 4. That was the time people came to picnic, hike, and fish. Hardy souls would even camp at various spots around the mountain.

Someone might even designate himself a fire marshal and move to the top of the mountain, where a little shack stood with a view of the whole range. If someone did that, he would also have a view of Eddie and Dauber moving around the mountainside. "Dauber, I think we'll leave our special haunts like Little Strawberry Lake and the falls. I can always remember the beauty and the sounds we heard here."

Just then, Eddie glanced down to see a piece of paper that had apparently fallen from someone's pack. He slid off Dauber and carefully grabbed the paper, which was blank. When they stopped to eat, Eddie listed on one side all the plants he had seen on this north side of the mountain. On the other side, he sketched a scene of Strawberry Falls. He tucked it all together with his poem and vowed that some way he would get some paper to record this trip.

*   *   *

In July, the ranchers in the upper John Day Valley kept their eyes on the mountain. As the last of the snow disappeared, the range appeared blue and solid. The summer light shaded the whole mountain, except for the one visible white spot on the right hand side which was west of Strawberry Lake. It was common to watch for this small glacier to fade away, but rarely was there enough prolonged heat for this to happen. On the Martin ranch, it would soon be time to begin haying. Extra crews passed through the valley, and the ranchers hired them to speed the job along.

Sarah Ann had not recovered from the loss of her son. She thought of Eddie daily. Not only was he a worker in the fields, but he often found time to help his mother out in the kitchen. As she got older, Sarah Ann did get extra help to feed the large crew. This year, she seemed to need the help more than ever. She believed Eddie could take care of himself, but she longed to see him one more time. *What if he never comes home?!* Her worries made her tired as she worked.

The rest of the family rarely mentioned Eddie now. Sarah Ann and Thomas sometimes wondered about him and filled their evening conversations with "what ifs" that had no answers. Evelyn missed her brother, but found if she mentioned him, no one seemed to pay attention. She needed to talk about her loss, but no one would let her.

She didn't know that her parents did discuss her future. She was an excellent student and would easily get accepted at the Portland Business School. Except for George and Eddie, the Martin boys had gone to school in Portland after high school. That was the reason Eddie was finishing up to get his high school diploma when he had the fight with Mr. Page. Ma and Pa were planning to send him to school in Portland.

Sarah Ann had always held high hopes for Eddie, scholastically. Of all the children, he showed the most promise with reading and writing. His interests were wide and varied, including everything but ranching. He found ranch work boring, and everyone bossed him around because he was the youngest. His temper would flare when told what to do. It seemed to Eddie that no one gave him credit for having any brains. Ma understood this, but she seemed to be the only one.

Eddie was just a toddler when Sarah Ann returned from her trip East to see her ailing mother. Not only did the trip change her, but it changed the way she reared her children. Eddie and Evelyn were recipients of their mother's forward thinking: voting rights for women, protection of wives from ill-tempered husbands, new laws for the age to marry. The children overheard their mother expressing her views. Eddie especially dove into her literature and newspaper articles to get his ideas. Sarah Ann was missing more than a son with Eddie's disappearance.

CHAPTER SEVEN

EDDIE SCRATCHED ANOTHER MARK on his self-made calendar and figured it must be the first of July. He imagined that folks in the Valley would be studying Strawberry Mountain for any remaining patches of snow. The view from the John Day River would be devoid of all that could be seen except for the one little glacier that clung to the shady spot under the top. Looking southwest, the top of Strawberry was in sight, about a day's climb away. By July 4th, young adventuring picnickers would be deciding to hike all the way to the top, just to prove they could do it. Chances of being spotted by someone who knew him and the story of him killing a man in a fight sent shudders through his chest. Eddie mounted Dauber and coaxed him toward the top of Strawberry.

After a couple of hours' hard riding, the lookout shack loomed before them. As expected, it was deserted and dry. If they were to stay here for a bit, water would have to be brought up from the little spring they had passed, or melted from the corner of the glacier on the west. Eddie dismounted and staked Dauber where he could feed, then explored the shack. Evidence that various little harmless critters had spent time here lay about the floor and in the corners. One handmade wooden box with a lid stored a few essentials, but the biggest treasure was a pad with directions for reporting a fire if spotted and blank paper for writing notes. Eddie removed some of the good blank paper from the pad and stashed it safely in his inside jacket pocket. With Dauber content on the back side of the lean-to, Eddie decided to spend the night in the shack. It was his first night under cover since leaving the Avery's barn over six weeks ago.

Three walls and a roof over his head did not give him a feeling of safety. Rather, it seemed confining and offered no means of escape. Eventually he did fall asleep, only to be awakened by a roll of thunder. From the top of the mountain one could hear a storm coming, feel the change in the air, and spot the strikes of lightning jutting about in the mountain range. As morning broke, he studied from the skyline down, looking for tell-tale plumes of smoke that would indicate a fire. Nothing could be seen today, but the value of having a fire watcher in this spot during the summer could be easily determined. Maybe one more night here would be safe, but moving on would be safer.

As Eddie gathered his pack, he heard Dauber give a soft whinny. Every muscle in his body tensed with fear. The sound of voices carried across the hillside. They would fall out of earshot, then break the sound waves as they came closer. Eddie saddled Dauber as quietly as possible, mounted up and headed down the south side of Strawberry. He just hoped he had left no signs of having occupied the lookout. More than that, he hoped no one had spotted Dauber, his beautiful pinto with the taupe colored spots. This was July 2nd, and he just wanted to put as much space as possible between the top of the mountain and himself. Heading down the south side was new territory for him—no lakes and waterfalls that he knew about. Dry virgin territory with unknown trails lay ahead.

CHAPTER EIGHT

MR. PAGE SHOWED SIGNS of improvement, and Dr. Froman, the new Prairie City doctor, assured him he would recover from the beating he had taken. He could be seen around town, walking with a limp and using a cane. He returned to teaching and finished his year at the school, but no one was surprised when he tenured his resignation to the school board and left town. Thomas and Sarah Ann offered to help him with his medical bills, feeling a certain responsibility for the injuries. Thomas did not tell anyone of the offer as he felt a Christian responsibility, but a personal one, not to be shared from the pulpit.

Sarah Ann honestly admitted to Thomas, "I am glad Mr. Page has moved on. Seeing him when we went to town reminded me of Eddie, his disappearance, how we had spent years trying to get him to curb his temper. I felt like a failure, and the brunt of gossip was more than I could bear."

"Sarah Ann, when a man, or woman for that matter, grows up, he or she is responsible for their own actions. One thing we did instill in Eddie was that knowledge. I'm sure he was prompted to run because standing up to the responsibility was more than he could handle. I believe he will make his own way in life. Maybe he will return to us, but we have to remember, he believes he killed a man. Living with that will take some hard thinking."

"Our boy has a good mind, Thomas. He is just not a farmer by nature. I expect he will be found doing something else with his life. I did think he might show up at Amy's in Idaho. After all, he headed east when he left."

"There's something I have not told you, Sarah Ann," confessed Thomas. "The day after Eddie left here, he spent the night at the Avery's. Paul rode down to tell me the next day. They tried to convince him to come down to town, but he stubbornly refused and took off up the mountain. Paul said he was not going to volunteer that information unless the sheriff asked him specifically. When he could see Page was going to recover, he just kept quiet. Forgive me for not sharing this information before this."

Sarah Ann was speechless. Her feelings were hurt. But after a time, she could understand Thomas's reasoning in keeping the information quiet. Again, she found herself hoping for a miracle.

* * *

Eddie knew a bit about the south side of
Strawberry Mountain, but the north side was his
side. It sloped to the John Day Valley. The
extensive water system that drained into the John
Day River came in part from the mountain. It was
the same looking from the south. Strawberry was
the highpoint and the water that flowed creek-by-
creek down the south side, filled the Malheur
River, Silvies Creek, and Malheur Lake. The Great
Sandy Desert lay between the Blue Mountains and
the high Cascades to the west. Eddie had heard
stories of men trying unsuccessfully to cross the
desert. But, he also knew the story of Mr. Fisk,
who brought his family into the John Day Valley
in 1859, settling near Strawberry Creek. In fact,
Fisk named the creek because the wild
strawberries were so plentiful. The mountain had
been called Mt. Logan back when the soldiers
were protecting settlers from the Piutes.

To get to Eastern Oregon, Fisk's wagons had
crossed from west to east, as his family had first
settled in northern California. The news of gold
drew them to the Eastern Oregon area, like so
many others. When the people couldn't live on
gold, they reverted to farming and ranching. The
youngest Fisk boy was pretty young when they

made the trip. He relayed tales of scarce water, unfriendly Indians, and harrowing crossings of the South Fork of the John Day.

"Well, if the family of Fisks made the trip across the desert from west to east, I should be able to make it from east to west. I think I'll get off this mountain as soon as I can, get into the town of Burns, and spend part of my saved money on some essentials," Eddie whispered to Dauber as he clicked his tongue with their "let's get going" signal.

From a clearing, he could see the white cone of Mt. Hood in the Cascades as it peeked slightly into view. The row of white-capped volcanoes that marched from Canada to California gave the residents of Central Oregon a glimpse of what one could find for scenery if moving west. There were only four or five spots where the naked eye could see the phenomenon. Spectacular as the view was, for Eddie, it could not compare to Strawberry Mountain, his friendly, beautiful peak that the residents of the Upper John Day Valley looked to for weather changes, season changes, grass for grazing, wild game for hunting, and wild food for the gathering. Tears began streaming, wetting his cheeks and making mud of his dusty face. A last picture embedded itself in his brain. The protection from his mountain was now a memory. The view he had enjoyed for the past eighteen years would remain clear in his mind, but chances of him ever seeing it again for real were pretty slim. Eddie wiped at the tears, the first he had uncontrollably shed since leaving the ranch two months ago. He had one goal: never to be caught by the law.

CHAPTER NINE

EDDIE STEERED HIS HORSE to the right and headed west. The terrain grew more rugged, and Dauber picked his way through brush and ledges of rock. It was evident this was not the easy way down from the mountain. When they came to a creek that was running north, Eddie realized he was off course. This had to be Canyon Creek, which headed back toward the John Day. The trusty compass was dug from the bottom of his pack for man and horse to get their bearings again. It was easy to see how wanderers could get lost in woods and mountains, only to be found much later, decomposed, where they had taken a fall or been attacked by a large animal.

Eddie figured they needed to climb to the top of the ridge he could see to the south to again be on their way out of the mountains. After about an hour, a good-sized huckleberry patch gained his attention, and in a picking frenzy, he turned his attention to something better than being lost on

Canyon Mountain. After filling his stomach, he put some in a rag in his pack where they would be squashed and turn into their own jam after their downhill ride.

Near the base of the mountain, Eddie spotted a ranch. Passing it by, he found the road that led into the Malheur Valley. He discovered a spot off the beaten path, near the creek, where he cleaned up a bit before making his way to Burns and civilization.

As he rode into town, he decided he should use a different name. People might not recognize his face, but Martins had been Eastern Oregon pioneers since the mid-1800s, and people might know the name. Eddie liked the first name of Jim. Then he thought of Drake, which was short and easy. He tossed Dauber's reins over the hitching rail near the dinky hotel and walked inside to inquire about a room.

Using his new name, Jim Drake, Eddie secured lodging and a place for Dauber and then strolled the main street, looking in windows, more to see how he looked than to peruse what was inside. He stopped at the general store to pick up scissors as he did not anticipate any joy in trimming his hair and whiskers with his hunting knife. He bought a new pencil and an envelope to complete his purchases at the store. His next stop was a restaurant called "Maude's Home Cooking," the end of a perfect day.

Eddie arranged for one more day at the hotel and for a tub for a bath. He didn't mind being the first and only person in the tub. With three older brothers, it seemed his bath always came after the "big boys" in the kitchen at the ranch. As the older siblings left home, the tub and even the whole house seemed less crowded. He imagined his parents feeling the emptiness of the place now that he was gone. One of these days, he would write his mother a letter, after feeling assured he was no longer a suspect for the law. He had heard of cases just being dropped after years of searching. He had also heard of suspects finally being found and brought to justice. Eddie knew all these stories because he liked to read so much. He located an old *Oregonian* in the lobby of the hotel and took time to devour it from beginning to end. There was no mention of the murder of school teacher Page from Prairie City.

Burns was a friendly enough place. People on the street tipped their hats as they passed by. Ranching and lumbering seemed to be the major occupations. There was a mill a few miles south of Burns that looked like a prospect for work. Eddie had not planned to stay here and work, but adding some money to his coffers held some appeal. Some workers lived at the mill, which would take care of the hotel bill if he could get on the crew.

When he inquired, the night custodian had just been promoted to a better paying job, so Eddie lucked out and went to work watching the mill at night. The turnover of employees brought strangers into camp regularly. It made Eddie nervous to get acquainted with each new worker. One evening, he overheard some conversation about John Day country. Men do talk about where they have been and what they have seen. Eddie discovered men gossiping just as much as women.

When the new man said, "Where are you from, Drake?" Eddie realized he would not only have to answer to his new name, he had to also be prepared to share some made-up background when people asked. Already, he could tell it would be important to always keep the story straight. The new man asked too many questions. Maybe he was just curious, but there was a shiftiness to his eyes, and they were too close together. Eddie's pa had always told him to watch out for a man whose eyes were close together. Close eyes seemed to go with pinched noses, but Pa never mentioned checking out the noses.

Everybody called the new guy Bud. One night after work as Eddie came on shift, Bud said, "Hey, Drake, how about a game of poker?"

"Sorry, the boss was real clear when he hired me not to socialize with the crew at night. So I guess I'm pretty well shot down for card playing. Thanks anyway," said Eddie as he slipped outside to make his rounds.

A card game with Bud would not be a good move. The Martins were never card players, especially the poker parties held in the Prairie City Pool Hall. Gambling was out, and friendly poker led to serious gambling, no two ways about it. Except for getting in fights, Eddie always followed the rules of the Martin house

The end of July, the camp cook quit and headed to The Dalles. He thought he would learn to smoke salmon from the Celilo Indians and go into business furnishing the markets in Portland. The boss offered "Jim Drake" the job of cooking for the camp. Eddie knew cooking would be tiresome, and hungry men would be hard to please, but the added pay was a good incentive, so he took the promotion. Mike, the current chef, gave him a couple of days of instruction before he took off. Eddie tried to remember all he had been taught. Then he remembered the tasks his mother had enlisted his help with—potato peeling, frying meat, flipping eggs—but best of all, she had taught him how to make pies, a real hit with the crew. "Thanks, Ma," he whispered at the end of the first week.

Bud wouldn't give up. "Now you can join the card game," he pressured.

"Sorry, I don't play."

"No worries; we'll teach you," Bud said with a wink. Eddie could find no way out. He did desire to be one of the regular guys. The first night wasn't too bad. The men explained the rules, and he even won a little money. The next time Bud invited him, Eddie was willing to take another lesson. At the end of two weeks, he figured it out. He was being taken. He could see the eagerness in the expressions of the men and sensed they would be winning big, and he would be broke.

The next night, Eddie feigned an upset stomach. Then he told the boss he would have to move on. "My sister, over in Idaho, is sick and the family needs me on the place to help out." The story was partially true: Amy had been sickly, but no one had written him to help. It was just a phony excuse to leave a trail to Idaho.

The boss noted that "Jim Drake" had received no mail, but he had a feeling this young man, a quiet good worker, needed to move on. So by the middle of August, Eddie headed west, after starting east, and was saved from the poker game. Bud shrugged when his mark left and set his mind to finding a more lucrative poker-playing greenhorn.

*   *   *

Eddie, the greenhorn, took a turn south after appearing to head east. The direction took him to Malheur Lake, a much larger lake than those he had visited on Strawberry Mountain. The banks were filled with little inlets, perfect for fish and small game. He moved from campsite to campsite, always breaking his pattern of camping. Many days he got by without making a fire as the weather still filled the days with warmth, and the bed role on oilcloth kept him comfortable at night. A lovely little skunk family came calling after Eddie stumbled over their home, making Eddie and Dauber not too pleasant to be around. They washed over and over in the lake and finally wore off the smell.

They met one of the best trout fishermen Eddie had ever seen. The old man was called Win, and he kept a permanent camp on the north side of the lake. He stored his smoked fish in a hand-hewn wooden box. His dried berries lasted most of the winter months. In the fall he would go to town and buy flour and baking powder to make biscuits all year. Eddie could see some of the chores he needed to do to be a successful camper. The two men shared food and the work of gathering it. They also shared ideas every evening at the campfire, but neither pried into the affairs of the other. Eddie was sure the old man had secrets to keep. Scars on his hands and arms plus a jumbo size welt Eddie had seen healed up across his back made Eddie curious, but neither of them volunteered information.

Eddie wrote some information in his pad of paper. He always signed his pages Jim Drake. Anyone who saw the little book would have no clue that it came from Eddie Martin.

His fishing partner knew the Malheur country and the great desert between the lake and the Cascades. He made maps for Eddie in his pad with estimates of distances and locations of water. When Win went to town one day, he offered to return with some of the supplies Eddie needed. Eddie shared money to buy flour and an extra canteen. Win was gone so long Eddie was afraid he had just ridden off with the money, or had had too much to drink at the saloon and told someone about the young fisherman who had joined him. After three days of waiting, Eddie packed up Dauber and gathered his own essentials, ready to head west with his new knowledge and the supplies he had.

Old Win appeared that evening. His apology for drinking too much and blabbing too much put Eddie on edge. The next morning he shook the fisherman's hand and said his good-byes. The fall weather was cooler for Dauber. "Well, old boy, let's see how long it takes us to put this Malheur desert between us and the Prairie City law." With a pat to his shoulder, Dauber took off on a slow trot.

CHAPTER TEN

"JIM DRAKE." He practiced the name, rolling it off his lips, pausing and trying accents. "*Jiiyum* Drake," slow and southern sounding. "I'm Jim . . . Jim Drake," spoken with authority. "James Drake, my man!" crisp and clipped like an Englishman.

In the end, he decided to give up on the accents and stick to what felt the most natural to him. The miles drug by slowly in the desert. "Jim Drake" talked to himself, talked to his horse, composed imaginary letters to his mother, thought up poems and then tried to remember them when he stopped to rest. By the time he retrieved his pencil and pad, they had escaped his mind. Rarely did he spot a bush or rock to provide protection for camping. He rationed his water with Dauber and hoped the wind would not pick up and bury them in a sand storm. According to fisherman Win's directions, he finally reached the Wagon Tire junction where the trails intersected, east-west, crossing north-south, and a bit of water in a swampy area.

Jim Drake planned to give Dauber a full day's rest and reorganize his pack. The choice was a good one, as they could see a storm racing from the west across the desert sky. Jim had never been so happy to have the Avery's oil cloth, as it became a tent on top to protect him from the rain, sand, and wind. When the howling stopped, and the pelting became an occasional drip, he saw that the little swampy place had filled with enough water for big drinks, for the removal of one dusty layer, and for filling both canteens. The wind helped to dry the wet bedroll and jacket so they could pack up and travel on without fear of mildew and moldy supplies. Jim created a nonsense poem as they rode on. He sang it to his own tune so he wouldn't forget.

The J D Lament

JD, the mountain man
Climbed the rocks
Fished the lakes
Talked to his horse
And let his brain run wild.

He left his beloved mountain
Left the woods
Left the chipmunks
And most of the trout
And let his brain run wild.

JD found himself in a desert
How did it happen?
Two months of lonely
The need to communicate
And he let his brain run wild.

Jim/Eddie sang his way across the desert with every ballad he knew, and new ones he created. He kept looking for the white cones in the Cascades. His intent to see them up close pushed him forward toward the various tree lines. After two weeks of solitude with Dauber, he rolled into a lumber camp. The work looked hard, but Jim figured he could drive a team pulling a wagon loaded with mammoth logs, the largest he had ever seen. The loggers all wore plaid flannel shirts, just like mountain men. Looking at the camp made Jim/Eddie think of home, even the books he used to read with his mother when he was a little boy. How strange the memories were and the occasions that caused him to have them. The loggers would work until snow-fly. Jim was again seen as a greenhorn. He pulled the chains that held the loads to the wagons. By night, every muscle ached. He could hardly drag his food from the plate to his mouth. Old timers eyed him and gave him a bad time about being too small to do the job.

They don't know that I got in a fight and beat a man so badly that he died, muttered Jim/Eddie. Then he realized he should put that out of his mind. What if he had a nightmare and spilled the beans? A tough logger and a murderer: not the reputation he wanted to establish. *So far, I would like to be a chef and a poet. I wonder what Pa would think of that if he knew I had finally decided on something to do with my life.*

Jim hung around hoping the cook would quit the camp, but winter arrived in the mountains, and camp closed due to the bad weather.

* * *

Jim prepared to head into the nearest little town down the west side of the mountains when Zeke Manning gave him a holler. "Hey, Jim, toss your stuff in my wagon and tie Dauber behind. I'll give you a lift down the hill, so to speak."

Jim took him up on the offer before he started to freeze up. Zeke had always been friendly. He was an old geezer who knew the ropes around lumbering. Jim wondered why he came to the hills and battled the hard work and bad weather. Maybe on the ride back to civilization, Zeke would spill his story.

If Zeke did the talking, Jim would not have to share his life story with the old man.

And talk he did. Jim enjoyed the listen because he had been a bit starved for conversation the past six months. Carefully watching his own words had changed him into an introvert. Now he was headed to Gold Beach with Zeke. There would be a house to share. He could help Zeke to get his house in order after being vacant all summer. He could help the widower fill the voids left there by the absence of his wife. Jim could imagine what it would be like back at the ranch if one of his parents passed. Obviously, he would never know about it if he had no communication with his family, but it just wasn't safe to take the chance. In his pack was the envelope he bought in Burns, waiting for the letter he planned to write one day.

Zeke was a church-going man. Jim felt obliged to join him on Sundays as it obviously pleased him to have company when he shook the preacher's hand. Jim took advantage of meeting people and building the story of his life, which seemed to go over pretty well. No one expected a murderer to be in church in the next seat in the pew, even one who had killed a person by accident.

Many houses in Gold Beach needed repair. Seacoast towns took a harder beating from the weather than the buildings in the eastern part of the state. Repairing them was no harder, though, and Jim had learned carpentry skills back on the ranch. Woodwork had been one skill his father had taught him that he enjoyed. He and his brother George had worked together on many projects, the one skill they both liked and could do without disagreeing.

Mrs. Benton needed someone to fix the hole in her roof before Gold Beach's storms arrived, so Jim was her man. She didn't pay much, but she always shared something fresh from her oven that he greatly enjoyed.

"You know what, Jim? My granddaughter is coming for a visit for Thanksgiving. She goes to school in Portland, and I don't see her very often. Maybe you and Zeke would like to pot luck a Thanksgiving dinner with us."

"That sounds real good, Mrs. Benton. I'll check with Zeke."

As Jim rode up the hill on Dauber, he began thinking. *I wonder where her granddaughter is from. Portland could be boarding school.* His brothers, Les and Lee, and sister Mary had all spent some time after high school studying in Portland. *Mrs. Benton's granddaughter could be from somewhere other than Portland, maybe close enough to the John Day Valley to have heard about the fight that caused a school teacher's death.* Jim knew he had to come up with an excuse to miss the holiday dinner. He was being forced to move on. Getting attached to these good people in Gold Beach presented a danger for which he was not prepared.

Jim sat in his room at Zeke's and finally scratched out a note to his mother. He put the envelope in his pack, ready to mail when the time seemed right.

*   *   *

In Prairie City, the apples had been picked and canned into applesauce, and the cattle were being fed from the hay wagon. It looked like a hard winter coming up, but the hardest thing at the Martin house was the absence of Eddie. It seemed that the hole in Sarah Ann's heart hardened up. She had avoided visits to town and neighbors, but it was time to get on with things. They would not be taking Eddie to school in Portland as planned, but they could begin plans for his younger sister, Evelyn.

Sarah Ann's health was slipping, although she did not say anything to Thomas about it as she did not want to worry him. She knew he missed Eddie as much as she did. He blamed himself for never being able to teach the boy to control his temper. It was like that game parents play with their memories when their children grow up and still have troubles, even when the troubles are of the offspring's own doing.

By Thanksgiving, when Mr. Page had recovered completely and accepted a teaching job elsewhere for the next year, the law dropped its search for Eddie Martin as Page refused to press charges. His embarrassment at a beating from a student drove him to try to forget it rather than make more of it. That's not to say he would not have loved to get back at Eddie if he could have found out where he was.

At church, folks finally stopped asking Sarah Ann and Thomas if they had heard from Eddie. They had not, and would not have said so if they had. Then one day Thomas picked up their mail in town. In with a few Christmas greetings was a letter for Sarah Ann without a return. Her trembling hands held the envelope for a long while before tearing the seal.

Dear Ma and Pa,

I know you have worried about me. Not a day passes that I don't think of you and the ranch. I have many regrets that I let my temper get the best of me. Pa always tried to teach me to hold it. If I had ever thought I could kill someone because of it, how different things could have been the past year. I will not tell you where I am or have been. Please do not try to write me or find me, because that would put me in a danger I am not prepared to face up to. Know that I love you both and will never forget what you taught me. I think you could be proud of me now.

Don't share this with the family. It would be too dangerous, as gossip is like a slimy eel that has a way of slipping around where it is not wanted.

You might like to know I have written a poem or two as Dauber and I moved around. We found lots to look at as we rarely had people to talk to. It's amazing what one can see when being quiet.

Do not expect to hear from me again. I can take care of myself just fine.

Love to you both.

Sarah Ann looked at the letter slipped into the handful of Christmas cards. A few people sent cards, and she received them from her relatives in the East. Anyone seeing her mail would have assumed it was all Christmas mail from New York. She realized Eddie had sent his note at just that time on purpose. She showed it to Thomas and then broke her own heart as she burned her evidence of Eddie in the kitchen stove, wishing she could tell him the important information that he did not really kill a man.

CHAPTER ELEVEN

JIM MADE HIS EXCUSES to Zeke about leaving before Thanksgiving. His comfort in Gold Beach came to an end. He asked Zeke to apologize to Mrs. Benton about leaving before meeting her granddaughter. How lovely it would have been to meet a pretty young girl, but he knew that would have to wait until he became established far away from Oregon.

He and Dauber rode over to the Rogue River and took the trail over the hills, past the Galice mines which were shut down due to weather. He was cold and weary when he rode into Ashland, another one-horse town on his way to nowhere, or somewhere; he didn't know which.

Jim tossed the reins over the rail in front of Red's general store and wandered in to take a look around. The pickle barrel next to the cash register drew his attention, something he had been missing since leaving home. Jim paid for the pickle and stood around until Red took notice and said, "Howdy there, stranger. Where you from?"

"I just rode in from the Redwoods," Jim lied. "Is there a place for lodging around here? I'm interested in some work for the winter as well."

Red ran a hand through his graying orange hair as he studied the young man. There was something in his straight mouth and gray eyes that made Red just a little nervous, but he couldn't place what it was. He was hesitant to send him to Millie's if he was a dangerous type. Millie ran a little boardinghouse and could take care of herself, so Red said, "Down the block is Millie's. She rents rooms on her second floor and sells the bread she makes from the street entrance. Last I heard she had room for one more boarder."

Anyone studying the young man would see he looked tired, tired in the eyes. He led his horse to a hitching post near a restaurant with a "home cookin'" sign in its window. He was reminded of his ma's meals back home, especially the apple pies. The regret in his expression could not be ignored. Jim checked the coins in his pocket before he ordered the chicken-fried steak with mashed potatoes. He took his time eating, lingered over a cup of tea, and surveyed the patrons in the cafe.

"Howdy, stranger, where'd you ride in from?" asked the man on the counter stool next to him.

"Rode in from the Redwoods a few days ago. Mining in California is pretty well petered out for me. I'm looking for other work."

"Millie Brown is looking for a handyman down at her place. You might give it a try. She takes in boarders and laundry, anything to keep the wolf from the door, but she needs help keeping up with the work when the boarding house is full. Sometimes she gets someone to work for room and board"

"Thanks," replied Jim. He left the cafe and led his horse on. He needed a place for Dauber as he had to keep the horse for now. He was still a man on the run.

For once, luck was with him. Millie Brown did indeed offer him a job in exchange for room and board. Jim knew he would stay just long enough to get through the winter and then move on. He didn't share this with Millie, but she had seen enough drifters to figure it out. He was not much more than a boy with a hungry, scared look, but she decided to give him a break.

CHAPTER TWELVE

MILLIE SHOWED JIM to the back room. A single wide bed filled it up. Several wall hooks invited Jim to hang his pack and his coat. The corner washstand sat under a small, cracked mirror. Jim thought it all looked fine, much better than a cold bedroll in the woods. He sat on the edge of the squeaky bed and anticipated where a little oil would improve a man's sleep. By morning, he had discovered a broken spring that had dug a sore spot in his back overnight.

At breakfast, Jim inquired where he could locate some wire and tools so he could fix the bed spring.

Millie eyed him and said, "If the bed spring is broken, plan to fix it on your own time. Today I need the halls swept out and the porch cleaned off. This place requires work to keep it running right. That's why you're here occupying the back room."

"Yes, ma'am," answered Jim. *So that's how it's going to be around here*, he thought to himself. *Well, I've got a warm room for winter so I've got no legitimate complaint.*

After a week of sweeping regularly, the boarding house looked acceptable. The porch, always clean of snow, looked like a good place to sit a spell in the winter sun. Equipment in the tool shed invited Jim to volunteer his services. "Say, Millie, there're some rolls of Robert's Ready Window Stripping in the shed. Do you have plans for them?"

"Oh, a traveling salesman talked me into buying that stuff to upgrade the place, but then he rode off and left me with something I had no way to install."

"I could put it up around your windows. We could try it on a couple and see how it works. It should catch the drafts. Winter would be a good time to try out the product," suggested Jim.

"Well, go to it," said Millie.

Jim started at the window in his little back room. After all, he could enjoy a draftless room just as much as any tenant. The job took longer than he expected, but he was pleased with the final result. Millie nodded approval but suggested he could work faster.

"Yes, ma'am."

*   *   *

Jim discovered he could install the weatherstripping better from the outside of the windows.

He took time to count the windows in Millie's house and figured how many days it would take to finish the work. He was hoping there would be the right amount of Robert's Ready Window Stripping to do the whole house. Millie's place had a lot of windows. There were three good-sized ones on the first floor, six on the second floor, and six more on the top floor.

Jim located a very tall ladder. He started at the top because he thought his skill as an installer would improve the more he practiced. As he worked his way around the house, townspeople watched with interest. Some wondered if he was available to do more houses. Jim thought he could see a possible winter business if Millie would sell him the unused weather-stripping.

"I guess so, Jim," said Millie. "You have things looking good around here, so you have time to work besides keeping up this place."

Jim began to think his life had something to offer. He began fixing Ed Mert's windows. They were looking good, and Mrs. Johns had asked him to do her house, too. Then he looked in the upstairs window at Ed's house. There was Ed's daughter changing her blouse. Jim could not look away fast enough without toppling from the ladder. Sophie Mert looked up, spotted him and gave a startled yell. Then Jim and ladder toppled together.

Innocent as it was, Jim garnered some gossip among the Ashland residents. Nine months of keeping to himself, avoiding news from places around the state, and now he was the brunt of jokes in the local saloon. His fame was spreading, and he did not want that to happen. Jim began looking around for a reason to move on. Millie sensed it.

People kept asking Jim to weather-strip their windows. If he said yes, there would usually be a wink and a comment that there were no pretty young girls behind their windows. The people were "funnin'," but Jim would turn red in the face every time.

When Sam Lawson stopped to spend a couple of nights at the boarding house, Millie had a feeling Jim would look toward Sam as a way to head east.

Sam Lawson stuck out his hand and said, "I'm Sam."

"Howdy," Jim replied as he shook the man's hand.

"I spotted that good-looking horse over at the stable and they said it was yours. You're Jim Drake, I presume."

"That's right, and the horse is mine—Dauber.

"Jim, I'm looking for someone experienced with horses, whole teams in fact. I have wheat land in the eastern part of Washington, an area known as the Palouse. If you're not committed to life in Ashland, how would you like to have a job working horses for me in the Palouse?"

Jim hesitated, but Sam said, "I'll be here a few days. Think it over and come talk to me if you have any questions."

He took a couple of days to consider the opportunity. He talked briefly to Millie who said, "Jim, I always knew you would move on. People here like you, but I see something in your eyes that says, 'I'm a man on the move.' I've known Sam quite a while, and I think he is a good person to hook up with, honest and fair. Take care of yourself and think of your friend Millie once in a while."

With that, Jim packed up his belongings, a few more than he came with as he had added some tools of his own, and went looking for Sam to accept his offer.

CHAPTER THIRTEEN

"LET ME TELL YOU about my plans," said Sam. "First, I need a man good with horses, and I think you may just be that man. I took a look at you with that horse of yours. No matter where you've been, you've taken care of your horse."

Jim nodded, "That's true."

"I have a piece of wheat property in the Palouse area of Washington. We're still using teams with our equipment, but a steam combine is on the horizon. In addition to more mechanization, there will always be need for horse-drawn equipment, mowing corners of the field, hauling small loads and equipment. A man on horseback tends to the irrigation of our property and moving small herds of cattle about. I just have a sixth sense that it would be the kind of work you could do well. Also, I need hands who live a quiet life, and I can tell you're not over-talkative."

"It sounds like my kind of job."

"Good. My first goal is to get to The Dalles and pick up a new team that Gus Plane is holding for me. We should be there by the end of the week, so if you are ready to leave, this is the day to say good-bye to Ashland."

Jim thought, *I don't know much about this man, but he doesn't know much about me either, so off we go.* He gave a wave to Millie, picked up Dauber at the livery, and climbed next to Sam in his wagon.

*   *   *

A chilly wind blew them up the pass, but later on the winter sun thawed them a bit. Sam knew places to stop and warm up. Jim wondered about his new companion but refrained from asking questions. Sam shared enough information to keep Jim content with their arrangement.

As Sam had promised, they picked up the new team in The Dalles. Jim agreed they were fine specimens of horseflesh. It would be a pleasure to work with them. They trailed the horses to Celilo, where they stopped for a break. Jim had seen pictures and heard stories of Celilo Falls. The Indians stood out on rickety-looking platforms built over the Columbia River and speared salmon. What a sight to behold!

After they tired of watching, Sam took them to one of the shack-like houses and traded for some smoked salmon. Jim, who had grown up on beef and pork, found a new love in salmon. The more he ate, the better it tasted. Sam chuckled and said he would earn a stomachache for his greediness. Jim felt embarrassed and wisely slowed up his eating. They took some packages of the smoked delicacy with them. Sam said it was for his missus and his daughter. Jim became curious, as this was the first time Sam had mentioned having a family. He asked no questions, though, as he didn't want to open a sharing session with the man. As always, Jim stayed private.

Travel up the gorge of the Columbia River made a windy trip. When they reached Arlington, a decision had to be made. They could cross the river by ferry, which would put them in Washington. It would be possible to stick to the Oregon side and continue east around the big bend where the Snake River met the Columbia. Sam and Jim talked it over, and they decided going around would be safer with the new team. It made their trip longer, but these horses were a real investment and Sam didn't want to take any chances with their safety.

Jim had seen a lot of dry flat country by the time they arrived in the Palouse. Wheat would sprout on the rolling hills, but Jim could see his love of mountains would be squelched here. His last longing look had been at the Wallows as they left Oregon for his new state. No doubt Washington would be a better state for a man on the run from the law in Oregon. Some days he was able to forget about Mr. Page lying in the dirt, but he never fell asleep without a memory of Strawberry Mountain, his landmark of protection.

Sam's missus was friendly but shooed Jim to the bunkhouse the first night they arrived at the wheat ranch. The second day, Sam came out to show him around.

"The barn is adequate for your horse and our new team. Let's call them Dolly and Fred, the names my daughter picked for them," Sam said. "As soon as you're comfortable with them, you can hitch them to some of the equipment around the place that we'll need to use them for. They need to be reliable by harvest time.

"Tomorrow we'll ride the borders of my property, see where the winter wheat is planted, the small area where we keep a few head of cattle, and the stream and two springs that we depend on. Pa Fleming, my wife's father, will show up in a few weeks to train you on what we do here. He homesteaded the land and ran the place until his daughter married me. Now he helps out with the jobs you will do, but he says he will retire and move to Spokane after this year, so I need a good replacement. Pay close attention to what he tells you. No one knows this property like he does."

Jim was beginning to see what this job would be. More men would be around for planting and harvesting, but he would be the general flunky for the rest of the year. He took his meals with the family until the big crew came. He was never encouraged to take part in their activities otherwise. He was suspicious that Sam was afraid he would spark interest in his daughter, and Sam and the missus had bigger plans for her future.

When the crew stayed on the place, Jim shard the bunkhouse and occasionally rode into Sprague for some weekend adventure. He found he was not much for carousing in the evening and feeling bad in the morning. It was as if his mother and father still had a hold on his behavior as the years passed by. It made him a good ranch hand for Sam, but eventually, Jim began to feel a need to move on.

A new century was just over the horizon. Sam had a new venture and Jim was a part of it. Several ranchers in the Palouse discovered land available in northern Idaho. The area was near Priest Lake. When the heat of the Palouse drove everyone except the workers to find respite, these affluent ranchers packed up their families and took them to Priest Lake for a summer holiday. Being farmers at heart, they grew wonderful gardens, kept a few animals, caught trout in the streams and the lake and stayed until the weather drove them home.

Sam found it hard to desert the summer property, so he proposed to Jim that he stay through the winter and take care of the place. Occasionally, he would be able to ride to Spokane for supplies and pick up "messages of civilization" as Sam called them.

Jim tried it for one year and liked it. Snowshoeing and hunting winter game reminded him of home in Oregon. The panhandle of Idaho provided the seasons and the mountains, all things Jim loved. The century turned and Jim decided he was home.

On one trip into Spokane, he found stacks of outdated newspapers in the back hall of the Davenport Hotel. He picked out the *Oregonians* and carried them to his room to peruse. Jim felt compelled to read the news of record, crimes, and obituaries. It was here that he found an obituary for Sarah Ann Manwaring Martin. He stopped reading as his life flooded before him. Of course, his mother was old enough to die, but Jim always pictured her stoking the fire in the square old kitchen to heat up a meal for the family.

He thought of the pain he had brought to them by running away. Then he imagined the pain they would have had if he had gone to jail. It troubled him to think of how he had disappointed his family.

CHAPTER FOURTEEN

HE PICTURED HOW on a winter day back in Prairie City, his parents and his sister would have been in town to pick up supplies. Pa and Evelyn would have gone to Marsh's to get flour and cornmeal, Evelyn to check out the latest newspaper, while Ma would go to the post counter and pick up the mail. When seeing the letter with no return, she would have slipped it into her pocket for safe keeping until they arrived home. Jim knew how it would have been for her.

When his mother received the letter he had written about three years ago, she would have opened it with trembling hands, trying to read the postmark, but to no avail. It was from Eddie, all right. She would recognize his handwriting and the way he said things. There was always a certain flair to his wording, not just the facts. Sarah Ann had secretly wished for him to be a writer, rather than a rancher, but Thomas was determined to arrange for his boys to own land to tend and animals to care for.

Sarah Ann would have tried to memorize the words her son had written before she burned them in the kitchen stove. It was a doubly sad day as she said good-bye to Eddie permanently, losing hope of ever seeing him again. It was reality to all the family except Evelyn, who craved the sight of her big brother, the one who had grown up as her playmate and protector.

*   *   *

Now it is really time to get on with my life, thought Jim as he packed up to get back to the lake. He did take time to look at some men getting driving lessons in a horseless carriage. He picked up some of the literature and sat in one of the vehicles to get the feel of it, very different from a wagon. He thought about giving up Dauber and going for an auto. Dauber was aging, but he knew it would be a hard change to make. Maybe on his next trip to town, he would look into the mechanics of automobiles to see if he would be able to figure out how to keep one operating. With that thought in mind, Jim headed home, north to Priest Lake, never again south to Oregon and his beloved Strawberry Mountain.

Sam had written with a date that his missus and her sister expected to arrive at the lake for their summer holiday. Sam now hired a cook to take over the hard work in the Palouse ranch kitchen during planting and harvesting. Sam's missus was industrious and she spent hours working on the Priest Lake place. Jim got the garden started and the beach cleaned up before she arrived. The winter driftwood was piled high, ready for beach fires when summer came. Sam's daughter was spending a year in Chicago studying the arts, or some such thing. Jim never asked as he still felt Sam wanted him to stay far from his daughter.

The last two weeks of August found Sam's whole family enjoying their vacation at the lake. Jim set up a campsite out on the point as the house was totally full of guests, including his room.

As fall approached, the guests began to leave, one by one. Sam's daughter returned to Chicago by train. Her friend, Emmie, and Emmie's mother decided to stay until snow-fly to take photographs of the area and hopefully of the winter animals. Jim was left in charge of Emmie and her mother, keeping them safe and comfortable. The mother did much of the cooking, which Jim enjoyed. As a bachelor, he was a good meal preparer, but the mother had a more sophisticated touch. However, Jim's time in the lumber camp as a cook had prepared him for western "home on the range" fare. Jim and the mother experimented in the kitchen as

Emmie took photos of winter birds and animals fattening themselves up for hibernation. The garden was put to bed, and the remaining crops were harvested, dried, stored, and even a few canned. Jim was again reminded of the kitchen back home when his mother took over the apple picking, applesauce canning, and apple pie baking.

Emmie took pictures, which she developed in the dark back room, a storage area with no windows. She also made drawings while sitting on the porch, facing east toward the morning sun. Jim was inspired to write some descriptions and some song lyrics to accompany her work.

"Emmie, do you mind if I write titles for your pictures?" asked Jim. "Sometimes I even want to write some words for my little ditties that would go with your pictures."

Then he proceeded to share his latest song:

"Baby Bobcat"
Did you see the baby bobcat?
Looking in your door?
He eyed that piece of meat
You dropped upon the floor.
We heard a little squeak,
A baby bobcat yowl.
We heard a little squeak
A baby bobcat yowl.

Jim described the baby bobcat, soft fur poking from his young ears, whiskers that were a little floppy, looking gentle, like an overgrown house cat:

Then he scooched back over the fence
With a quick backward glance,
And we heard a little squeak,
A baby bobcat yowl.

Jim did his writing by the light from coal oil lamps after his other work was finished.

Emmie seemed to like the little songs and descriptions. She also seemed to like Jim himself. There was a quietness about him that appealed to her, although here in the Priest Lake woods, there was no competition for her interest. The time they spent together as he escorted her away from the homestead and acted as her protector gave them time for a friendship to grow.

Like most young ladies, Emmie was curious about Jim. He certainly was well-read for a young man, but he never mentioned his schooling. She wondered where he had done his reading, but he never shared that most of it was behind the apple tree back home with his mother's books and magazines. He could never relate his time in the Prairie City school where he ended his education by punching the teacher in a fit of rage, so hard that the man died. When Emmie expressed her curiosity, Jim changed the subject and usually remembered chores that needed his attention. Emmie found this mysterious but was too polite to go any further by questioning him directly. However, it didn't keep her from asking her mother what she had figured out about Jim while they worked together in the kitchen.

"I find him to be a good cook. He understands how food should be prepared. His specialty is apple pie. Not many men have the knack to create a great pie. They're usually too liberal with the spices, work the crust too long so it becomes tough, and ignore the artistic crimping around each pie they create. If I ever opened a restaurant, I would hire Jim as my bakery chef at the drop of a hat." Her mother's praises were wonderful to hear but did not answer the questions that simmered away in Emmie's brain.

CHAPTER FIFTEEN

EMMIE AND HER MOTHER seemed in no hurry to leave the lake, even though cold weather would be coming soon. Jim was pretty sure they weren't prepared with winter clothing or the stamina for snowshoeing. He began to wonder what his responsibilities would be in caring for Sam's house guests. His normal routine was to hunker down with a supply of books and magazines that he would bring in about the end of October with an ample supply of food. Keeping things refrigerated from November 1 through March 15 was an easy fix in this north mountain country.

Jim found himself thinking even more of his mother during this turn of the century year. If he could go home, it would be to confirm that he continued his reading even though his desire to study law was out of the question. He also wished he could have shown her what a fine apple pie he could make after years of watching her in the kitchen.

He knew the rest of the family would be putting him out of their minds as they would have been embarrassed by his stupid behavior. His little sister Evelyn might feel differently, but she was just a girl. His pa had tried valiantly to teach him to control his temper. Pa loved him, but he would feel as if he had failed to rear his son properly.

Ma's lessons remained with him. He thought of her every time he read a book or passed by a church. He felt he was cut from a different warp of cloth than the rest of the family. So one more time, he convinced himself he had made the right decision to leave home and not return. These were his usual thoughts as he rode down lake to Coolin to pick up mail and newspapers.

A letter from Sam gave permission for Emmie and her mother to stay on as long as they wanted. Jim was surprised, but not displeased by Sam's decision. He felt there must be something more to the reasons for them staying, but then he had mysteries of his own so would not pry into theirs. The general store saved old newspapers for him to carry home. First he would read them, then create paper logs to start the fires with the bulk of them. Occasionally, there would be a newspaper from Oregon, which Jim would devour with a passion. Emmie always wondered why he had such a fierce interest in Oregon.

* * *

In November, Jim bagged a turkey, scalded the bird, picked the feathers down to the very last pinfeather, and cleaned away the buckshot. He then presented his handiwork to Emmie's mother, who began plans for a Thanksgiving feast. Jim received his assignment of two pies, one squash and one apple. Emmie's mother realized she would have to parboil this bird to get it tender.

"Jim, please call me Fran. I consider us equals in the kitchen and would like to eliminate this formality we've established," said Emmie's mother.

"Well, sure. I'd like that," replied Jim. Fran was not as old as Sarah Ann, but she was "a mother in a kitchen," something he related to his hidden life from Strawberry Mountain.

They invited old Ned Rose who lived down lake to join them for their feast. It was so successful they all planned to get together for a Christmas dinner. Jim realized Emmie and Fran would be around the rest of the year as he listened to the talk. The real conversation began after old Ned said his thanks and headed home. The three of them cleared the dishes and put away the leftovers. A glance out the window over the sink as Jim was washing dishes showed him a whirling white. He alerted the ladies.

"Fran, Emmie, I think we're about to have a mountain storm. With ice on the lake and the howling wind, we soon won't know where land begins and water ends. I think I better get the animals herded into the barn where the hay is stored, if you'll excuse me from this dishwashing."

"Go, go!" urged Fran. "Do you need our help?"

"Not necessary," he said. "Just keep the fire going; check on the wood supply. I expect we will be hunkered down here for a few days."

After the stock were tended to, Jim came in to warm up. They all settled before the fire with the pleasure of warmth and the contentment of having enjoyed a wonderful meal. There was also a touch of apprehension and excitement to the upcoming storm. Jim learned Emmie and Fran were no strangers to bad weather as they related tales of their winters in Iowa, Nebraska, and Wisconsin, all places they had lived before Emmie's father passed on.

"Now, what about you?" they asked. Jim begged off, saying he was too tired to stay up any longer, and he knew he would need to be up early in the morning to shovel them out. He went off to his room to figure how to answer the next time he was cornered with questions about his past. That old worry of how people would react if they knew they were sharing quarters with someone who had killed a man. Another night of fitful sleep awaited Jim.

*   *   *

Spring. Jim wrote another letter to Sam just to clarify his position and duties. Emmie continued her photography and artwork through the cold weather. She could make animal tracks in the snow look like a painting. Jim watched her splash a bit of purple paint onto a snow picture and turn it into magic. He read every piece of literature in the house and composed his own stories about the woodland creatures hiding in the snow.

Spring seemed slow in coming as Jim and Emmie looked for the first buttercups. Even when the little yellow cup-shaped flowers peeked through new green grass, snow flurries could be anticipated to cover them over again. When the major stormy weather finally seemed to be over, Jim, Emmie, and Fran began to face the facts. The end of winter meant Fran and her daughter would be heading to their old home in the Midwest. The winter mail deliveries had brought the news that Mr. Randall's affairs were settled, and Fran was needed back home to close the household and business. The estate waited for her to come accept it.

Fran was worried about just what she would do as a widow with some money but not enough to last the rest of her life. Emmie needed to finish her education and share her artistic talents. She had corresponded with the art school connected with the Museum of Art in Omaha, Nebraska, In addition to a show, they were interested in a teacher for children who visited the museum. It seemed to Jim that Emmie's life was headed for success. As glad as he was for her, he realized how much he would miss their jaunts into the woods, her pictures, and his poems. He even realized he would miss baking apple pies with Fran.

Jim headed down lake to make arrangements for the two women to head east. He got the train schedules, ticket prices, and some newspapers to read to bring them up on current events. One of the papers was an *Oregonian* from the first week in March. Jim stopped his reading halfway through. For the second time he spotted his mother's obituary, which he did not want to read.

Fran wondered about Jim's change in attitude. She thought maybe he was thinking about missing them when they headed home. Jim and Emmie had become close friends, and Fran didn't object to their association.

"Say, Jim, what are your plans when we leave?" asked Fran.

"Clean up the property and get it ready for Sam's family," mumbled Jim. He was not sharing any extra words on this conversation, but Fran was not about to quit her inquiries.

"If we leave April 15, you will have a lot of quiet time, doing all your own cooking, spading up the garden . . . or is that what you like to do?"

"Fran, sometimes I think I should move on. As much as I love living in the mountains, the future here is limited. I'll end up living like old Ned. He has a good life, but I think a man needs a family to have a happy life." Jim surprised himself with this statement. It was something he believed but had never expressed to anyone.

"I've been thinking, Jim. How would you like to accompany us home to Nebraska? My place is near the Missouri River—no mountains, but good country. My place is not big enough to support a farmer, but I'm thinking of opening a restaurant. I would need your help as chief pie baker. Give it some thought. It would be a change for you. You're a young man who should step into the new century with a goal. Think about it. This would be the right time to let Sam know you're leaving to escort us home." Fran made a persuasive argument, and Jim planned to give it some thought.

Before the ladies headed east, Jim had some time to escort Emmie around the countryside.

Spring was popping in small spots as the snow began to disappear. They bundled up and took the boat across the lake one warm day. Emmie was never without her sketch pad, drawing in pencil, then carrying the pictures home where she added soft pastel colors. He especially liked the rainbow trout and the steelhead that fishermen caught. Sometimes she drew them swimming in the shallow fishing holes on the west side of the lake. When she finished her artwork, the fish scales fairly glistened like little mirrors in the sunlight. Jim was excited for her to be taking on a new career teaching the children who came to visit the Omaha museum. She promised she would start her art show with the bobcat picture and Jim's poem. He tried not to express too much pleasure, but getting a piece of his poetry on display made him proud enough to bust his buttons.

*   *   *

"Hello, Sam. This is Jim Drake. Everything is fine here at the place on the lake, but I think it is time for me to move on. Fran has offered me a job at her place in Nebraska after I accompany her and Emmie back home. I'll really miss the mountains of Idaho, but a new century means new things to do."

"Jim, I don't want to lose you, but I've always known you would want to move on one day."

Then Jim asked the question he knew had to be asked: "Would you be interested in taking Dauber?" He's still a good horse, but there are a lot of miles under his saddle. I'll look into shipping my saddle on the train. If that doesn't work out, I will leave it here for you."

Jim could hardly believe the call to Sam had gone so well. It made him aware of the pile of chores waiting for him to do to get the little ranch buttoned up for its owner. He needed to find a home for the chickens if he left before Sam got a replacement. Bobcats would soon make dinner of his black and white leghorns. Old Ned might take them down to his place just because he liked the eggs.

"Fran, I just talked to Sam. He's willing to let me out of my caretaking contract so I can escort you ladies back to civilization. Of course, you understand, I've never really been to civilization."

"You'll become Nebraska-sophisticated before you know it, Jim! I'm really excited about our plans!" said Fran. "This lake and mountain life is what you know, and you love it, but I see your interest in Emmie's art, and I know that you read stories and poetry by the oil lamp in your room at night. Take a couple of years to expand yourself and see what you're really like."

Fran turned her head toward him as she left the room. "Let's get packed and on that train out of Spokane, and I'll share my plans with you," she finished.

Jim had buttoned down the little ranch for Sam, arranged for Dauber's care, and helped the ladies with their heavy packing. Leaving Dauber was the most difficult. Jim had ridden him since he was a young man known as Eddie from Eastern Oregon. He had known this day would come, but the difficulty of it was immense. Last of all, Jim packed his saddle and his bag of clothes and paperwork. He lined the bottom of the case with a layer of newspapers, one page where the obituary of Sarah Ann Martin was included. No one seeing the paper would know she was his mother, but it was Jim's only connection to the past, except for his memories.

* * *

Emmie and Fran were excited to get over the Rocky Mountains and view the plains. Miles of flat land felt like home. Any trees they saw had young green leaves and even some blossoms. Jim craned his neck to see conifers with needles, but mostly the deciduous varieties were in evidence. As usual, Jim had read about the flora of the area east of the continental divide, so he was not surprised or homesick for the mountains and the evergreens.

When Fran's husband died, he left their small home and farm and a building in town on a busy corner in Lincoln. Fran saw the corner as a place of business for the future. Fran and her husband had envisioned a small art shop that could feature Emmie's work. They would have expanded into a gift shop, with jewelry, gloves, scarves, and household decorations. Plans changed when Emmie's father became ill and passed. Fran lacked enough capital to stock a store. Then Emmie had received the offer from the museum in Omaha which was too good to pass up.

CHAPTER SIXTEEN

FRAN BUSIED HERSELF back in her Nebraska home. She helped Emmie pack and move her treasures to Omaha. The art show was successful. Visitors to the museum flocked to the art department to see the Priest Lake drawings. These Midwesterners were eager to learn about the West. Since the time of Teddy Roosevelt, the citizens of the United States had concerned themselves with setting up parks and designating land for the populace. The homesteaders were mostly miners who destroyed land with dredging, cattlemen and sheep herders who did not get along, and cowboys who caused trouble with the Indians. Homesteading became unpopular in the United States.

The first Christmas in Nebraska, Emmie came home and the three of them relived their year before at Priest Lake. Jim gave Emmie a Kodak Brownie camera. The new cameras could have the film cartridge removed and sent for developing, instead of returning the whole camera to the company to get the pictures. Jim thought it would be helpful to her in her work at the museum.

Fran and Jim found themselves slipping into restaurant talk. Emmie went off to draw pictures. Jim still spent lots of time reading and wanted to create a place for people to read and discuss the news. Fran thought people would read instead of ordering food. They decided to try a restaurant and reading room.

Jim's lonely years had been filled with what he read in the news. Now he found the news a source of gaining friends who agreed with him and being challenged by those who disagreed. He always remembered how his attempt to write a political paper had pushed him into the disastrous fight with his teacher, and turned him into a killer. Jim was a different man now. The world was a different place. Automobiles, electric lights, indoor plumbing, political news that spanned the world. He found himself fascinated with what was going on around him. He pictured Eastern Oregon as the backward area he had thought it to be when he grew up there.

Fran decided to use her property on the corner of Cottnier Street as a neighborhood coffee shop. She served breakfast and lunch and stayed open long enough to promote afternoon coffee, tea, and pie. When Emmie came home for a visit, she made an advertising sign that also mentioned Jim's apple pie. Jim Drake had never pictured himself as a baker or a restaurant worker, but Fran needed him and paid him well for his addition to the business.

The highway through town passed Fran's corner. Automobiles were replacing buggies, but Fran provided parking for both modes of transportation. Jim always found himself amazed at her business ability. By 1902, the little restaurant was running just fine.

Jim decided he should move into a place of his own. The money was coming in, and as always, he squirreled it away for safe keeping. They hired a waitress to help at the Blue Cup as well as a fast order cook so they could stay open for evening diners. Jim knew he needed to leave Fran's because every time Emmie came home, he found himself wishing she would stay. He knew she would never give up her art career, and he was never going to match the kind of partner she would need. Their time at Priest Lake was merely a passing fancy. They both knew it.

CHAPTER SEVENTEEN

FRAN AND JIM HIRED a waitress named Kathleen. Her Irish parents had come to America in 1904. They were wise enough to leave New York and head west, but Nebraska was west enough for them. By 1905 the whole family was working, and Kathleen took the job at the Blue Cup Diner. She knew how to cook if needed; she was cheerful and industrious. Her blue eyes sparkled when she talked to the customers. On sunny days her hair glistened red-gold when she came to work.

Jim was smitten with Kathleen. After five years in Nebraska, he was of an age to need a lady friend. He had forced himself into a lonely state since leaving Priest Lake. He had never wanted to be a farmer. The restaurant business actually appealed to him. What a surprise! He supposed no one was still searching for him as a murderer, but his fight with Mr. Page always held a spot in his brain. He did discover he could take Kathleen out for a movie and enjoy the whole evening without glancing over his shoulder. He had been unable to do that while living in the Pacific Northwest.

* * *

Fran and Jim introduced the popular new hamburger to their cuisine. The Blue Cup Diner became "the place to go" for it in Lincoln. No matter what was new, the stand-by apple pie brought the customers in.

Kathleen knew a bit about Irish politics but didn't discuss them with Jim and was happy to agree with him about the news in the United States. They made a good couple, and Jim decided to ask her to marry him. He was older than Kathleen, but she felt comfortable having him as her protector. Jim felt the same way about himself. No longer was he the younger brother whose opinions never mattered.

They were married in 1912. Jim was a young 35, kept his face cleanly shaved with his Gillette razor and had his hair trimmed regularly at the barber shop just down the street from the Blue Cup Diner. As Fran turned over more of the business to Jim, he became known as a businessman in Lincoln. Rarely did he think about his experiences in Oregon. He assumed the law was no longer looking for him.

Then one day, a couple he had known from Prairie City stopped for lunch. They were on a road trip from Chicago to Oregon. They were friendly and chatted about their trip, even thinking the restaurant owner looked like someone they knew.

Prickles made their way down the back of Jim's neck as he turned the customers over to Kathleen. Of course, they left before they remembered who he looked like, but he figured they would come up with his name about fifty miles down the road. This was the day Jim decided he should share his past with Kathleen. Possibly she would not want a man of his character as the father of her children.

Jim chose a Sunday evening to have the discussion and share the old secret. He was nervous and irritable. Kathleen had noticed his restlessness during church and sensed something was bothering him.

They sat at the kitchen table after dinner, each with a piece of pecan pie, something new to be added to the restaurant menu. Jim told the story, beginning with his life on the ranch, his temper, his fight with Mr. Page, and his classmate Clint coming to tell them that the teacher had died. He told her how he decided to run, how he spent time on Strawberry Mountain and then said good-bye to the mountain and his life on the ranch. He told her how he spent the next years always looking over his shoulder and never opening up to people. He confided that even Fran did not know about his past, but bless her heart, she had always taken him at face value. "I think she thought anyone who could bake a proper apple pie had to be a good person," Jim told Kathleen.

"Stop," whispered Kathleen as she put her hand on his arm. "Tell me what you choose to, but it will go no farther from my lips. Fran has trusted you, and I do too. I could share our family's sorrows from the old country, but there is no need. It just helps me to be a proper wife to you."

Jim looked at the adorable Kathleen and wondered how he could be so lucky. She made the nagging sorrow disappear. Monday morning would be the best day he had wakened to since before the turn of the century.

CHAPTER EIGHTEEN

MATTHEW SEAN DRAKE'S BIRTHDAY was March 16, 1915. Round and chubby for a newborn, his golden red hair was the highlight of his portrait which Emmie painted when she came up to Lincoln for a visit. "Imagine having a painting of our child for the living room wall!" Kathleen exclaimed. Then Emmie took a photo of the painting and made copies for all the family to carry in their wallets. This reminded Jim of his childhood when his parents had hired a photographer to record the whole family for a velvet covered album. He wondered if the album was still there and if they had left his picture in it.

Shortly after the joy of the birth, Jim became obsessed with the war effort and the gassing of soldiers by the Germans. "Even though I'm nearly forty years old, I am young enough to join the army and for once, there is something worth getting mad enough about to really fight. For once, I can unleash my temper on someone who deserves it. Kathleen, I'm going to war. The more of us who fight for right, the sooner we will all come home. Matthew deserves a father willing to stand up for his convictions. I am that man."

Tears stained Kathleen's cheeks as she held her young son, but she knew Jim well enough to know he had made the decision. She also believed this fight might relieve him of what had nagged him all these years.

* * *

Jim hated what the Germans were doing, how they fought in this war. His information came from his voracious reading of the newspapers. He pictured himself with a rifle, taking aim at the enemy, sniping from behind bushes, like hunting had been back on the ranch in Oregon. His wool uniform, heavy and scratchy, kept out the cold, and his wide-brimmed hat identified him as a new recruit.

Instead of target shots at the enemy, the division of American soldiers found themselves crawling through the mud with other allies, hoping to avoid the gassing from the Germans. At the end his tour, Jim was taken to a British hospital area where the troops were treated for the gassing. Captain Smithworth, a British soldier and ex-mining engineer who had spent time in the states and Canada supervised the treatment, one he had learned when working the mines. Jim felt close to the man and very grateful for his care. He was shipped home, never able to take out his hatred on the enemy, but realizing how much he despised the killing of men, even his enemies.

Finally, the war ended, and Jim, Kathleen, and Matthew devoted themselves to running the restaurant. A lawyer drew up an agreement between Fran and Jim, half for each of them. One day, Emmie would inherit her mother's portion.

When the barbershop went out of business, Jim saw an opportunity, to enlarge the Blue Cup Diner. The evening meals included entertainment. Sometimes the music made one section seem like a dance club. Money was good, and Jim thought about adding another location. When he discussed this with Kathleen, she pointed out that times were really changing. Skirts were shorter, liquor was flowing, women were voting, and she thought owning more restaurants would put them into a lifestyle they would not enjoy.

Jim reminisced about his father, the rancher back in Eastern Oregon who grabbed land when it came available. He was determined to have land to provide for his sons as they became ranchers. Jim had never wanted the piece of land or the commitment to farming that came with it. Maybe his son Matthew would feel the same way about owning restaurants. Maybe he and Kathleen should choose their own path and let Matthew do the same.

He also thought about his mother. He knew if his she were still alive, she would have been thrilled about women's suffrage but would have wondered why it took so long. Jim's life as a child kept coming back to him. Having kept it buried for so long must be why he was having these thoughts.

CHAPTER NINETEEN

"KATHLEEN, I'VE BEEN THINKING ABOUT a retirement vacation. Matthew has really taken hold of the restaurant business. Our remodel of the Blue Cup Diner with its reading room and fine dining area certainly proved successful. I would be happy to leave Matthew in charge so we could take a road trip. The '37 Packard for sale at the used car lot looks like a prize. We've saved enough gas stamps to get necessary fuel. I say, let's head west. I want to show you some real mountains, especially Strawberry Mountain. We could slip in and out of Prairie City without being noticed. What do you think?"

Jim was greeted with silence. Kathleen felt like she did when he decided to go to war, that he had made the decision because it was what he thought was best for him. She wondered if he had considered that she might not want to see mountains. What if he was recognized by someone after all these years and the sheriff still wanted him? Maybe just wanted to embarrass him? Then she looked closely at her husband and realized he was bringing closure to his life with this planned trip. She took a breath and said, "Jim, I think the mountains of the west have been waiting for me since I came from Ireland. Let's do it." Kathleen gave her approval because that is what good wives did. Back in 1915, Jim Drake had picked his perfect partner.

*   *   *

Many of the roads the Drakes traveled were not paved, but the main ones were. After they came into Prairie City, they headed east and left the highway about two miles up the road. The look of the property had changed in the past forty years. Jim slowed down when he saw a little girl standing in her yard, watching them stir up the dust as they drove by. He backed the car and stuck his head out the window. "I'm looking for the Martin place," he said. "Do you know how to get there?"

"My name is Martin. Are you looking for us?"

"Well, who lives down that lane over there?"

"Oh, Hansons live there. My Aunt Evelyn is a Hanson."

"Thank you very much. I think that's who we are looking for," said Jim.

He turned to his wife and said, "Kathleen, that's my childhood home at the end of this lane. My stomach is full of butterflies. I think I'm sorry I came. But please look at the mountain. Is it as beautiful as you thought it would be?"

"Yes, Jim. I can see why you loved it. What beautiful protection it provided when you needed it," answered Kathleen as they wheeled the Packard over the log bridge that spanned the John Day River.

CHAPTER TWENTY

EVELYN LOOKED OUT the back porch door as she heard a car drive up. Nigel had gone to Ontario to sell a few head of cattle. He expected to stay over as he would have to stick around until the paperwork was completed. She did not recognize the car in the backyard. She noted the license plate was not an Oregon one.

"Look, Kathleen. There's my Strawberry Mountain. Is it what you expected? You can see the glacier on the right. It never melts completely, even in hot summers. Is it amazing how blue it looks, not like any of the mountains we have crossed on our trip here."

"Well, this is a pretty valley, Jim. I really liked the view of it as we came in from Baker City and over that Dixie Mountain pass. I imagine you're having some special thoughts after all the years of looking over your shoulder and thinking you could never come back here again." Kathleen was thinking this was how she sometimes felt when she remembered Ireland. Of course, she came to the United States as a young woman without any fear of being chased by the law.

"Someone's coming out of the house. Is it your sister?"

Jim's attention was drawn to a small middle-aged woman coming down the steps. "May I help you?" asked Evelyn. Strangers rarely came down the lane as it was a dead end in front of the house. There was no recognition in her voice.

Jim took in the look of her, a bit like he remembered his mother. She wore a cotton house dress with a typical apron to protect it from the drips and grease of kitchen work. Her voice still had the familiar ring of his younger sister. He thought how strange it was that he could recognize her voice after 45 years.

Evelyn did not recognize the man unfolding his body to exit the strange car. He said, "I am looking for the Martin place. Is this it?"

Why would he call this the Martin place? It had been Hanson's since she and Nigel were married. Of course, it was the Martin place before that. "My name is Hanson, but my maiden name was Martin."

"I haven't been here for many years . . ." Jim was interrupted by Evelyn's gasp. She heard his voice again, and she knew this was Eddie. The two of them stood a few feet apart and stared to take in the moment. Kathleen opened her door on the passenger side of the car. The sound of it broke the spell.

"I thought you were dead," said Evelyn.

"I was afraid to come home. I knew I was an embarrassment to the family. How could they bear to have a murderer as an offspring? How could I stand to be sent to prison for killing a man?"

"But, Eddie, you didn't kill Mr. Page! He recovered from the beating and even went back to teaching school. We had no way to let you know," Evelyn replied. "Wait just a minute. I have the clipping from the Oregonian retracting their story that Mr. Page had died. It will take me just a minute to find it in the back of my first diary."

She returned with the article and handed it to Eddie.

Mr. Page, who was beaten by Ed Martin at Prairie City, in Grant County, instead of dying, as was reported, has recovered, and has resumed his position at the Prairie City School as the senior class instructor."
Wednesday, January 13, 1898, Oregonian (Portland, Oregon)

Eddie read the notice in silence. He passed it to Kathleen, who came forward, taking his hand in hers. She could feel the sweat on his palm as he comprehended the message of Evelyn's words and the newspaper clipping he held in his hand.

"Evelyn, this is my wife Kathleen." Jim's manners took over.

"How do you do?" said Evelyn. "Please come in. I just made some lemonade. You must be thirsty from your drive. Somehow we need to catch up on our lives during the 20th century."

* * *

During the next three hours, conversation and lemonade filled the kitchen where the Martin children had grown up. Evelyn's husband Nigel had taken their son with him to sell the cows. There was no one to interrupt the catching-up conversation between brother and sister.

"When Pa died, we made attempts to find you. The cash on hand was divided between the children. You were due to receive a little over $3000. After seven years, the search was officially closed and the money was split between the remaining children," reported Evelyn.

She showed Jim and Kathleen current pictures of the family. "You must stay over, meet my husband and son, and have a family dinner with George, Lee, Mary and their families," urged Evelyn.

"No, that's not going to happen. There may be hard feelings and no reason to open them up after all these years. I need time to wrap my head around the fact that I didn't kill a man. My life would have been so different if I had known, but I wouldn't have met and married my Kathleen, had our son Matt, and so much more. In fact, Evelyn, I would like you to keep my visit a secret between us, just like we did with our pranks when we were kids." Jim's decision was firm. He and Kathleen had discussed this on the trip and agreed on passing through Prairie City with no fanfare.

The brother, sister, and sister-in-law stood in the driveway and hugged each other, putting closure to their unanswered questions. Evelyn returned to her kitchen and then dissolved in tears. Kathleen and Jim rode up the lane in silence. As they turned toward the highway, they could see the little girl who had directed them earlier standing in her yard. According to Evelyn, she was George's granddaughter, Annie Martin.

As they headed down the road, Kathleen said, "Jim, when I came to the United States I waved good-bye to the Atlantic Ocean, never wanting to see so much water again. But now, we're close to the Pacific Ocean. I want you to take me there before we go home. Then I can say I have been coast-to-coast.

"It's over 300 miles to the coast, Kathleen!" Then Jim/Eddie looked across the seat at his still pretty Irish wife and figured she had certainly earned a trip to the coast. They were ready to start a late-life adventure, without the specter of a dead man in the background.

"Oh, why not! You deserve a trip to the Pacific Ocean. Let's head west!" said Jim as he pulled the car to the shoulder of the highway and took up his road map.

"We'll roll through Prairie City, so take one last look at Strawberry Mountain. Tonight we'll get to Prineville and stay at the Ocheco Hotel, if it's still there. Tomorrow we'll head for Eugene. You'll see mountains like you have never seen before. The Three-fingered Jack, The Three Sisters, Mount Jefferson. That's all I remember from forty years ago. But see here," Jim pointed to the map to show Kathleen, "after that we will head west to the ocean."

Kathleen studied the map as Jim pulled back onto the road. His enthusiasm seemed to overshadow the long-awaited and powerful visit with his sister at the ranch.

They spent two days driving the coast highway to Astoria where they turned east for their drive up the Columbia River. They were like pioneers in reverse.

After they passed famous Mt. Hood, Jim said, "I want to show you the Indians fishing at Celilo

Falls. I read the government is taking about building a hydroelectric dam that will flood the falls. It makes me heartsick to think of it. This is the first place I ate smoked salmon."

After some silence, Kathleen said, "Shall I learn to call you Eddie?"

"No," said Jim. "I'll put a document in with our wills for Matt's information, but Eddie is part of the past. Jim Drake is the successful businessman from Nebraska."

"When we get home, Matt and his wife will have a surprise for us." Kathleen smiled. "They'll be making plans for their baby, due before Christmas. Matt shared that news with me just before we left but didn't want the news to interfere with our trip."

Eddie hesitated for a moment, then pressed his foot to the accelerator. Grandpa Jim needed to get home.

A MESSAGE FROM THE AUTHOR

The Strawberry Mountain Series is set in the upper John Day Valley, surrounded by the Blue Mountains. As one looks south, prominent Strawberry Mountain captures the view with its height and beauty. The stories are inspired by my ancestors and the stories I imagined for them. All eight of my great grandparents came to the John Day Valley in the last half of the 1800s. I introduced one great grandmother, Sarah Ann Manwaring, into the series using her real name. After that, I took the liberty of changing many names as the stories became only my imagination. *By the River* is what I think her life might have been had we known her well.

The same is true of *Letters from the Little Red Box*. I was inspired by a 100 year old pack of letters. As an only child and eavesdropper, I heard fascinating family stories which I stored in my memory bank. Today, it only takes a small reminder to reinvent another story to be told. For example, the hand-painted perfume bottle that is found in the first two books, a letter that was written, but never mailed, a large print Bible, and so much more that is stored in files and cabinets in my home.

Readers of the first two books often ask, "Whatever happened to the youngest son who rode away? *Eddie* is the answer to that question, and is more of my imagination of what could have been. I enjoyed being able to share with the reader my memories of trips to the Strawberry wilderness and the dreams I had as I studied the mountain from my front porch and yard. Eddie is one more cog in the wheel of the Strawberry Mountain Series.

Please watch for the next book, *The Annie Martin Stories.*

63849239R00072

Made in the USA
Lexington, KY
19 May 2017